Mars

Sharon Callen

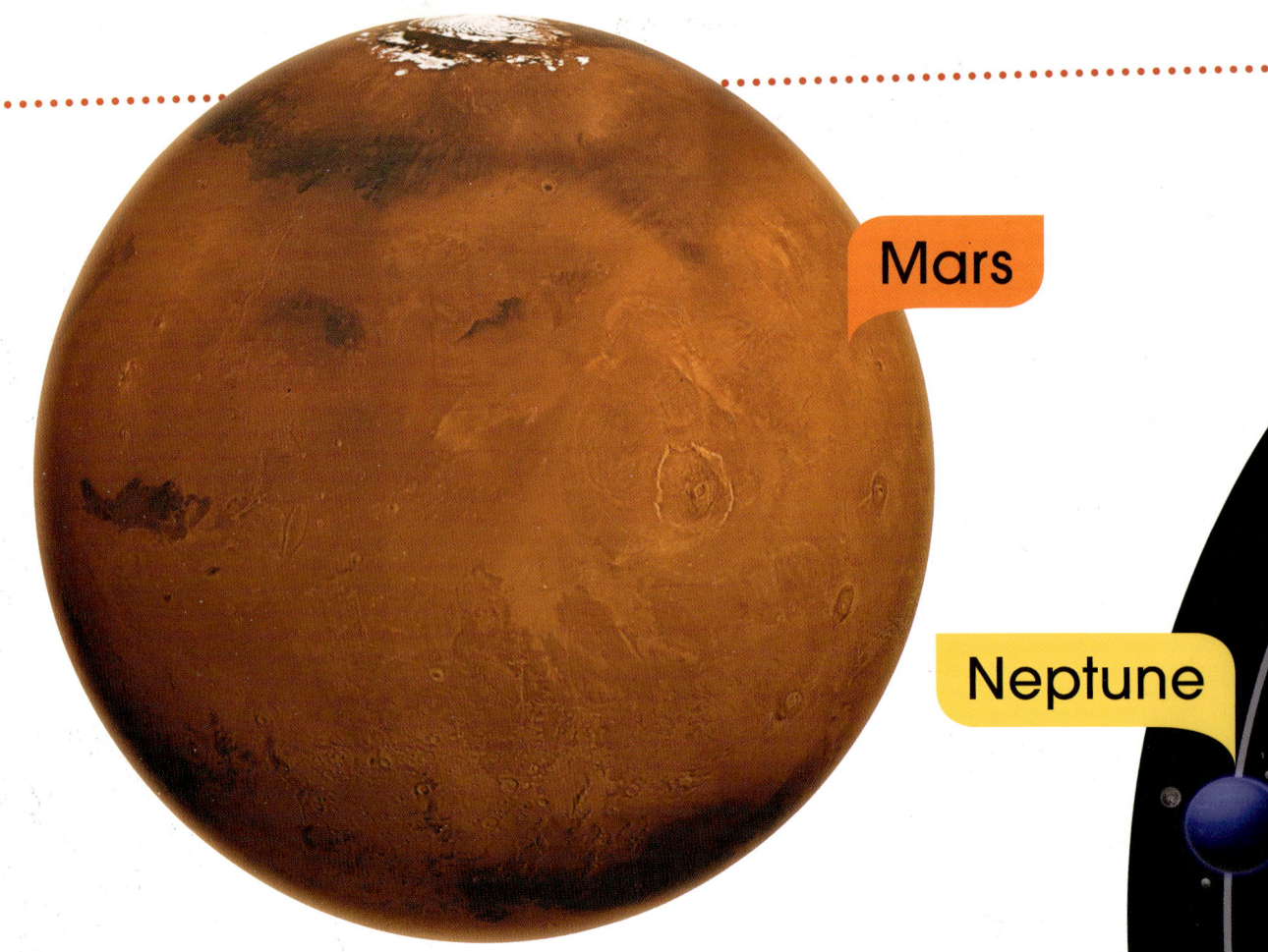

Mars

Neptune

The Solar System

Mars is part of the solar system.

The solar system has eight planets.

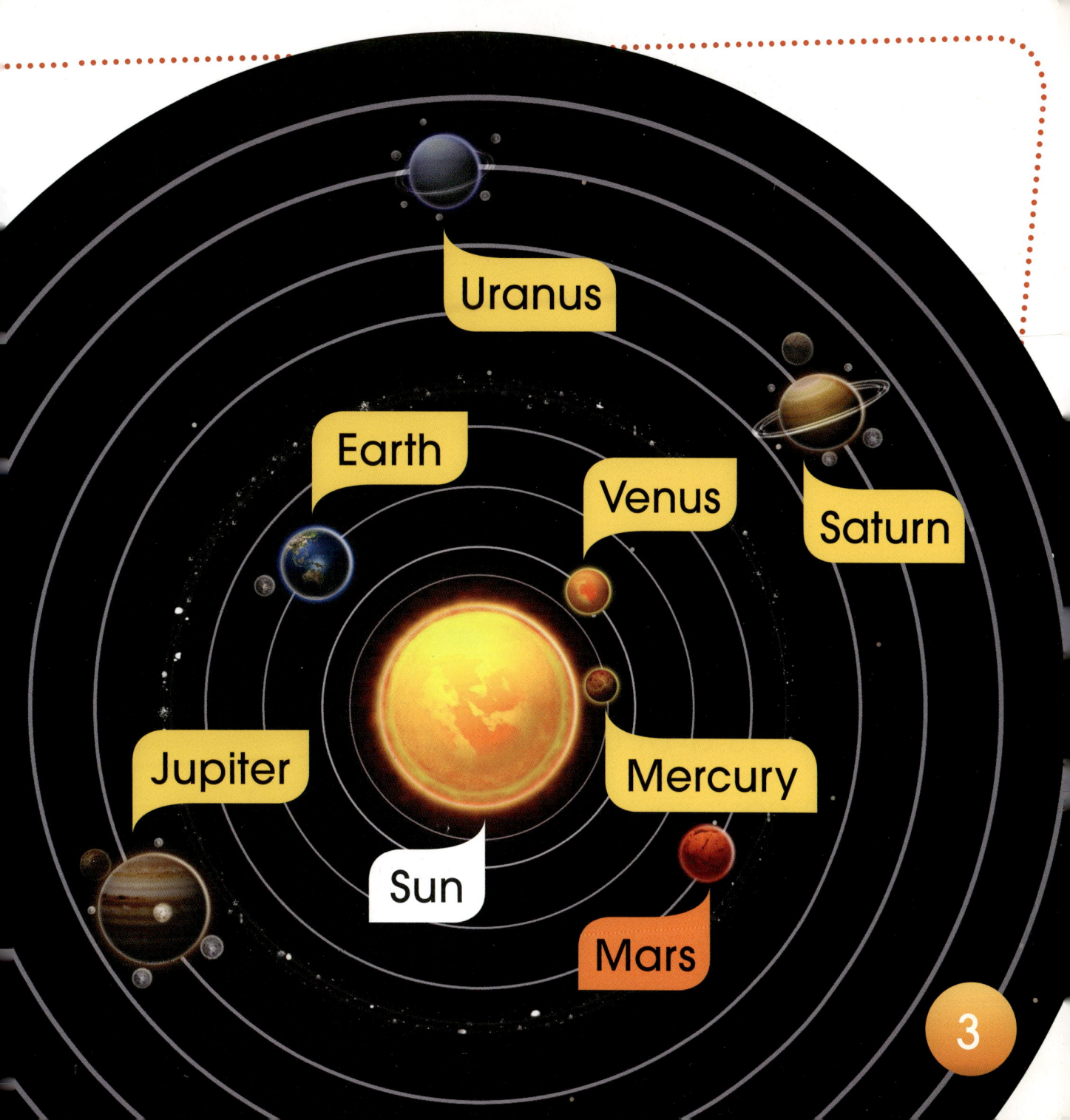

3

Mars

Mars is a beautiful planet.

It is covered in red dust, which makes it look very red.

People cannot live on Mars.

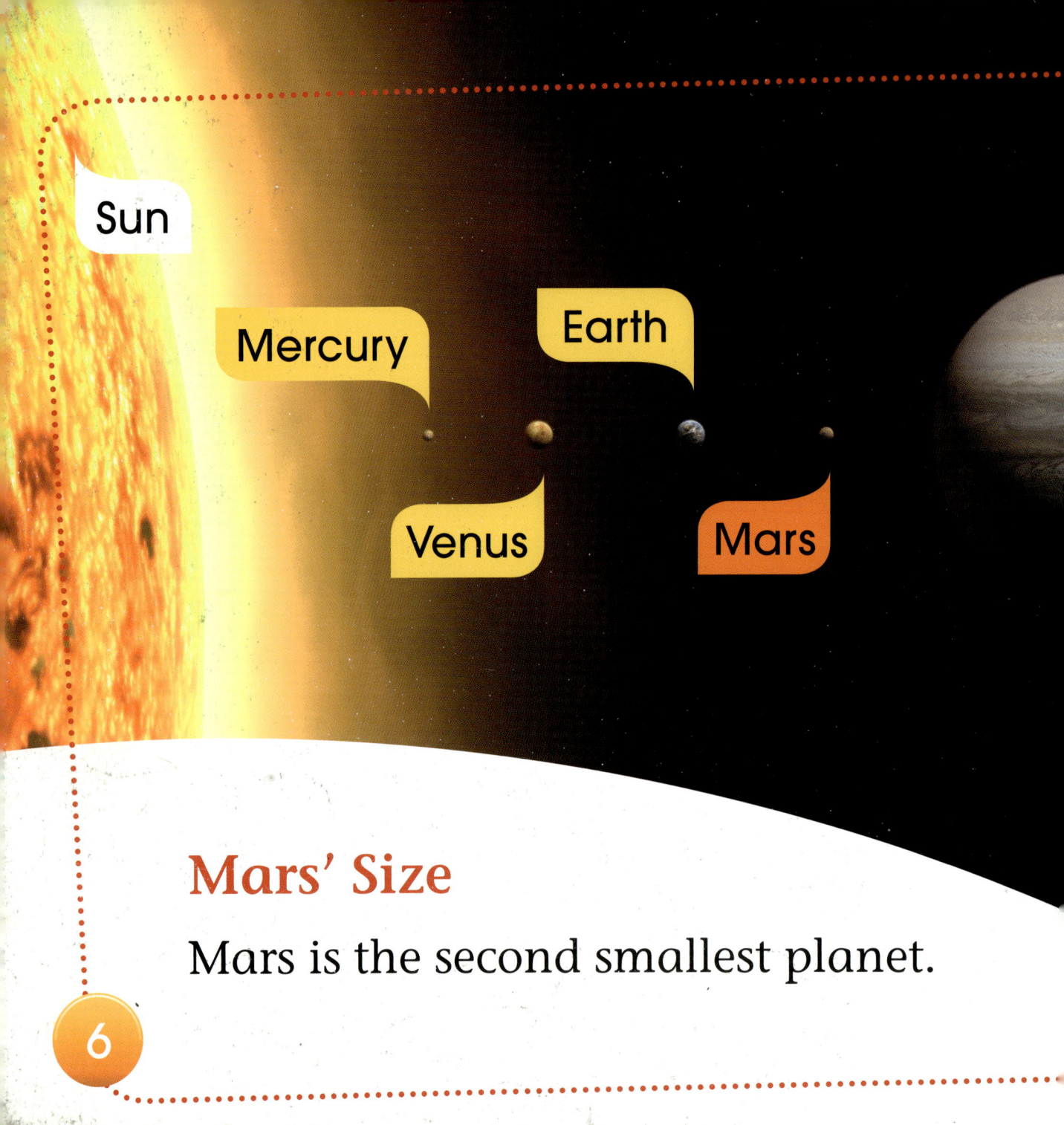

Sun

Mercury

Venus

Earth

Mars

Mars' Size

Mars is the second smallest planet.

Mars' Features

Mars is made up of rocks, dust, and ice.

It has mountains, valleys, and plains but no oceans.

Mars' Moons

Mars has two small moons.

They are very gray and rocky.

They are called Deimos and Phobos.

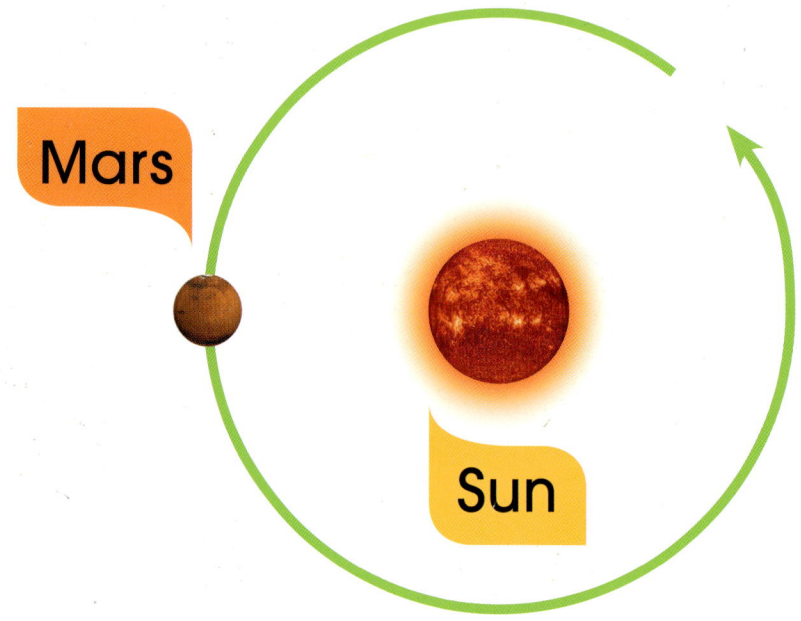

Day and Night

Mars has days and nights.

It is daytime on the part of Mars that faces the Sun.

It is nighttime on the part of Mars that faces away from the Sun.

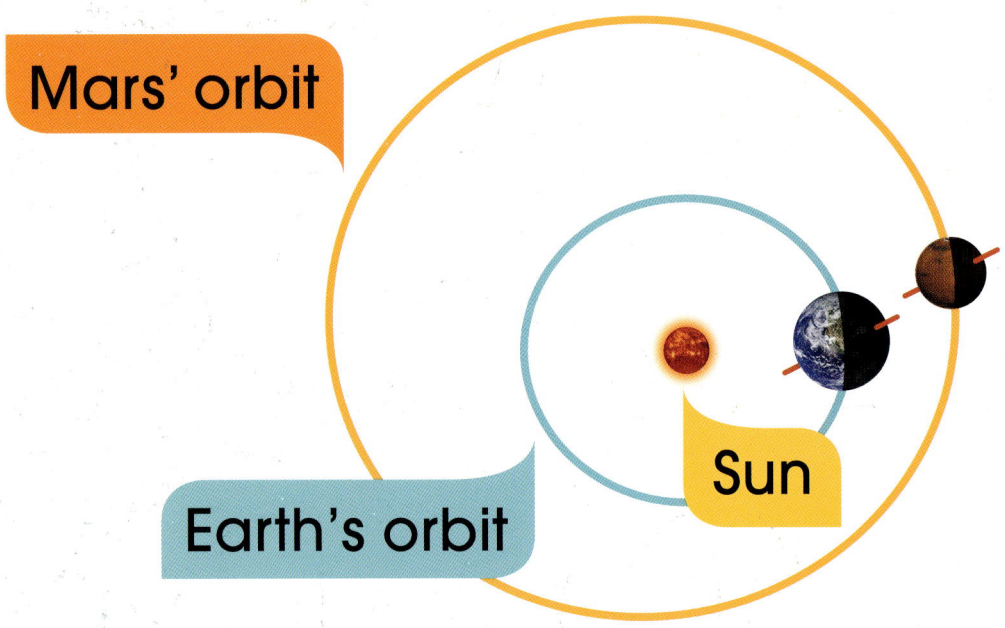

Mars' orbit

Earth's orbit

Sun

Mars' Orbit

Mars spins around the Sun.

Mars takes nearly 687 days to orbit the Sun.

That's nearly two years of your life!

15

INDEX